NEW HAVEN PUBLIC LIBRARY

3 5000 09309 7581

W9-ALL-680

Thanksgiving
at the Tappletons'

For Jer, who made my wishbone wish come true
—E.S.

Thanks to Katie, Krystal, Ian, and Aaron for excellent
modeling, and to "Ma Tappleton" Alisoun for
modeling and arranging it all
—M.L.

Thanksgiving at the Tappletons'
Text copyright © 1982 by Eileen Spinelli Illustrations copyright © 2003 by Megan Lloyd
Manufactured in China. All rights reserved. www.harperchildrens.com

Library of Congress Cataloging-in-Publication Data
Spinelli, Eileen.
Thanksgiving at the Tappletons' / written by Eileen Spinelli ; illustrated by Megan Lloyd.
p.   cm
Originally published: New York : J.B. Lippincott, © 1982.
Summary: When calamity stalks every step of the preparations for the Tappletons'
Thanksgiving dinner, they realize there is more to Thanksgiving than turkey and
trimmings.
ISBN 0-06-008670-X — ISBN 0-06-008671-8 (lib. bdg.)
[1. Thanksgiving Day—Fiction. 2. Family life—Fiction. 3. Humorous stories.]
I. Lloyd, Megan, ill. II. Title.
PZ7.S7566 Th 2003   2002017296
[E]—dc21   CIP
                                                                                                          AC

Typography by Al Cetta ❖ 1 2 3 4 5 6 7 8 9 10
Newly Illustrated Edition First published by Addison-Wesley Publishing Company.

NEW HAVEN FREE PUBLIC LIBRARY
133 ELM STREET
NEW HAVEN, CT 06510

Thanksgiving
at the Tappletons'

Written by Eileen Spinelli

Illustrated by Megan Lloyd

■ HARPERCOLLINS PUBLISHERS

E SPINELLI
Spinelli, Eileen
Thanksgiving at the
    Tappletons'

35000093097581 Children's

Thanksgiving at the Tappletons' was always a big day.
Thanksgiving at the Tappletons' meant, of course, the
Tappleton family: Mr. Tappleton, Mrs. Tappleton, Jenny
Tappleton, Kenny Tappleton . . .
And Grandmother and Grandfather Tappleton, and
Aunt Hetta and Uncle Fritz, and most certainly, of course . . .
the turkey and the trimmings.

It was still dark when Mrs. Tappleton lit the oven
and took the big turkey out of the refrigerator. Just then
someone knocked at the kitchen door.

It was Mike the milkman.

"Good morning, Mrs. Tappleton. I thought you might like
some eggnog."

As Mrs. Tappleton reached for the eggnog . . .

. . . the turkey slipped from under her arm. Now, on a
warmer day this might not have been a problem. But this
Thanksgiving Day was quite cold, and the step was covered
with ice. Before she or Mike could even think, the turkey
had slithered into the yard.

"Hurry!" screamed Mrs. Tappleton. "STOP THAT
TURKEY!"

The milkman chased the turkey . . . Mrs. Tappleton
chased the milkman . . . and the turkey slid down the hill
into the pond.

Plop! Splash!

It bubbled out of sight.

When Mr. Tappleton came down to breakfast, he took a long sniff.

"I don't smell turkey," he said to his wife.

"Of course you don't smell turkey," she replied. "You have a cold."

"I don't have a cold," he insisted.

Mrs. Tappleton shook some pepper in the air. Her husband sneezed.

"See," she said, "you *do* have a cold."

After breakfast Mr. Tappleton put on his coat and scarf and hat and gloves.

"I'm going to the bakery to buy our pies."

"Wear your boots," she said. "I know for a fact it is quite slippery out today."

Simms' bakery was so crowded, the line reached out onto the sidewalk.

Mr. Tappleton hated to wait in long lines. So he went to the diner for a cup of coffee.

By the time he got back, the long line was gone . . . and so were the pies.

Mr. Tappleton was afraid to go home with nothing.

"Two boxes tied up with string, please," he said.

Mrs. Simms stared at him.

"You mean two *empty* boxes?"

"That's right."

"My, they feel light," remarked Mrs. Tappleton.

"Certainly they are light," retorted Mr. Tappleton. "Mrs. Simms prides herself on how light her pies are."

Mrs. Tappleton set the table. She called to her son.

"Kenny, you may make the salad. There's lettuce in the crisper, and carrots and radishes, too."

Kenny's mouth fell open. Just yesterday he had emptied the crisper and fed all the vegetables to the rabbits in Mr. Butterworth's class.

How could he tell his mother? He couldn't.

So he covered the empty salad bowl with aluminum foil and stuck it in the back of the refrigerator.

When the others went to pick up the relatives at the train station, Jenny stayed behind to mash the potatoes. Every year this was her job. "This year," she thought, "I'll make them even better. I'll use the mixer."

Just as Jenny flicked on the switch, the phone rang. It was her best friend, Nora. Jenny loved to talk. Jenny talked and talked and talked to Nora, and she might still be talking today . . .

. . . had not a wet *glump* of something hit her on the back of
the head. She turned to see what it was. *Splat!* Another
flump hit her in the face.

The mixer was going wild, and mashed potatoes were flying everywhere. Without even saying good-bye to Nora, Jenny hung up the phone, scrubbed her face, and wiped mashed potatoes from nearly everything in the kitchen. She finished just as the others came back.

Uncle Fritz patted his stomach. "I'm hungry," he said.

Grandfather Tappleton laughed. "I'm as hungry as an
elephant."

Everyone sat down at the table. It was a Tappleton
tradition for Grandmother to say the Thanksgiving prayer.

"As soon as the turkey is ready. . . ." She smiled.

"I'm as hungry as *two* elephants," said Grandfather.

Mr. Tappleton went to the oven. "I'll get the turkey
now." He opened the oven door.

"THE TURKEY IS GONE!"

Mr. Tappleton searched on the table and under the table and in every kitchen cabinet.

He looked in the sink and in the broom closet.
"I can't find the turkey anywhere."

Mrs. Tappleton told them how their fine turkey had slipped out the door and down the steps and across the yard and down the street and—*plop! splash!*—into the pond.

"So much for the turkey," said Uncle Fritz.

"Never mind," said Aunt Hetta good-naturedly. "We'll fill up on the trimmings."

"I'll get the salad," Jenny announced. "Then Grandmother can say the prayer."

Jenny set the bowl on the table and peeled off the aluminum foil.

Everyone stared at the salad that was not there.

"I fed the rabbits at school," confessed Kenny.

"So much for the salad," said Uncle Fritz.

"I'm as hungry as *three* elephants." Grandfather sighed.

Kenny jumped up. "We'll have Jenny's mashed potatoes." He brought the pot from the kitchen and lifted the lid.

"I was on the phone," said Jenny meekly, "and the mixer went wild."

"So much for the potatoes," said Uncle Fritz.

"I'm as hungry as *four* elephants," Grandfather declared.

"The pies!" cried Mrs. Tappleton. "I'll get the pies!"

Mrs. Tappleton brought in the boxes, set them down, and untied the string.

"You brought home two empty boxes!" She glared at Mr. Tappleton, who covered his ears.

"*Five* elephants!" groaned Grandfather.

The dining room was quiet. Everyone looked down at the empty table.

Uncle Fritz muttered something, but it could not be heard above the rumble of his stomach.

A tear rolled down Jenny's cheek.

"No Thanksgiving dinner," she sniffled.

"Nothing to say a prayer for." Kenny sighed.

Grandmother smiled. "Of course there is something. There is more to Thanksgiving than a turkey and trimmings."

And then Grandmother Tappleton asked everyone to bow their heads and to hold hands around the dining room table.

And this is the Thanksgiving prayer she said:

"Turkeys come and turkeys go
And trimmings can be lost, we know.
But we're together,
That's what matters—
Not what's served upon the platters.
Amen."

"That was a wonderful prayer," said Aunt Hetta.

Mrs. Tappleton jumped up. "We have liverwurst and cheese in the refrigerator."

"I'll help fix the sandwiches," offered Mr. Tappleton.

Jenny wiped her tear away. "I'll get the pickles."

Kenny laughed. "I'll open a jar of applesauce for dessert."

And so the Tappletons had their Thanksgiving dinner after all.

Uncle Fritz's stomach stopped rumbling, and Grandfather Tappleton ate enough to feed *six* elephants.

In fact, everyone had plenty to eat. But most of all . . .

. . . they had each other.

MAR   2004